THE STORY OF DOCTOR DOLITTLE

by HUGH LOFTING

#3 Doctor Dolittle's Great Adventure

Adapted by Diane Namm

Illustrated by John Kanzler

Sterling Publishing Co., Inc.
New York

Library of Congress Cataloging-in-Publication Data Available

10   9   8   7   6   5   4   3   2   1

Published by Sterling Publishing Co., Inc.
387 Park Avenue South, New York, NY 10016
Copyright © 2007 by Sterling Publishing Co., Inc.
Illustrations © 2007 by John Kanzler
Distributed in Canada by Sterling Publishing
^{c}/o Canadian Manda Group, 165 Dufferin Street
Toronto, Ontario, Canada M6K 3H6
Distributed in the United Kingdom by GMC Distribution Services
Castle Place, 166 High Street, Lewes, East Sussex, England BN7 1XU
Distributed in Australia by Capricorn Link (Australia) Pty. Ltd.
P.O. Box 704, Windsor, NSW 2756, Australia

Printed in China
All rights reserved

Sterling ISBN-13: 978-1-4027-4122-7
          ISBN-10: 1-4027-4122-7

For information about custom editions, special sales, premium and
corporate purchases, please contact Sterling Special Sales
Department at 800-805-5489 or specialsales@sterlingpub.com.

Contents

Are We There Yet?

Six weeks had passed since
Doctor Dolittle and his
animal friends set sail
across the sea to Africa.
Would they ever find
Circus Crocodile's home?
The animals were worried—
except for Chee-Chee the
monkey, who was fast asleep.

"I'm hungry," oinked Gub-Gub the pig.

"I'm thirsty," quacked Dab-Dab the duck.

"I'm homesick," barked Jip the dog.

"Turn back," squawked Polynesia
the parrot.

"Impossible!" said the doctor.
"We promised Circus Crocodile
we would bring him home.
We have a job to do!"

"We won't find my home,"
said Circus Crocodile.
"Yes, we will!"
the others said.

"We will look harder for land,"
said the doctor.
"We'll all help,"
the animals vowed.

They looked north and
south and east and west.
"Uh-oh!" said the doctor.
"What is it?" Crocodile asked.

"It's a storm!"
the doctor shouted.

"Hold on tight!"
he told his crew.

Chee-Chee woke up.

He looked around.

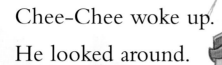

"Are we there yet?"

Shipwrecked!

It rained for many hours.
The ship tossed and
turned all day.
Then it got stuck
on a sandbar.
"We are here!"
Doctor Dolittle cried.

"You are home at last!"
he added, with excitement.
"I don't think so," said
Crocodile, shaking his head.

"This must be it,"
said Doctor Dolittle.
"I know it's not,"
Crocodile said sadly.

"Then we will set sail
and search again," the doctor said.
Just then, a great big wave
washed over the ship.

Their ship floated out to sea.

"How will we get back
to Puddleby?" Jip asked.

"We can't row all the way there!"

Crocodile started to cry.

"How will I find my family?"

"I'll think of something,"
Doctor Dolittle said.

Soon it began to get dark.

"I'm cold," quacked Dab-Dab.

"I'm hungry," oinked Gub-Gub.

Then they heard a strange noise.

"I'm scared," said Chee-Chee.

Jip barked at the bushes.

"Don't worry," said Doctor Dolittle.

"Let's just take a look."

It was a royal messenger!

"What can we do for you, sir?"

Doctor Dolittle asked.

"The island king

wishes to see you,"

the royal messenger said.

A Very Un-Welcome

"What brings you to our island?"
asked the island king.
Doctor Dolittle explained, but
the king did not believe him.
"Talking animals!
Homesick crocodiles!
What nonsense! Lock them up!"
shouted the king.

"What do we do now?"
Chee-Chee asked.
"I have a plan,"
Polynesia said.
She hopped out the window
and flew away!

Polynesia flew right to
the king's royal hut.
"There it is!" she squawked.

Hanging on the wall,
behind the king's sleeping guards,
was the key
that would free her friends.

"Hurray for Polynesia!"

the animals all cheered.

"Quick!" she said,

"No time for that!

We must escape now,

before the king wakes up!"

The Monkey Bridge

They ran far, far away,

following the beat of happy drums.

The sound led them

to a village of monkeys!

"We come as friends," said the

doctor in proper monkey-speak.

"Wonderful," said the monkey-king.

"You're just in time for soup!"

"Welcome, friends! Eat and enjoy!"
the monkey-king said.
Suddenly, the drummers
played a warning beat.

"Uh oh," said the monkey-king.

"The island king is coming!"

"We must go," said Doctor Dolittle.

"We'll help you,"

said the monkey-king.

They ran until they came to a cliff.

It looked like all was lost.

"Don't worry," the monkey king said.

"Hand to tail! Tail to hand!"

The monkeys made a bridge!
Doctor Dolittle and his friends
crossed safely to the other side.
"I know this place," said Crocodile.

"Little Crocodile!" someone called.

"Mother!" Crocodile shouted.

"You're home at last!" she said.

"Hurray for Doctor Dolittle!"
said Crocodile. "I knew you
would bring me home."

Doctor Dolittle simply smiled.